September 2 2006

For Megan,
Enjoy the ABCs
of the Jersey Shore.
Happy Birthday!
Best wishes,

Frank Finale

A Gull's Story

A Tale of Learning about Life, the Shore, and the ABCs

For my grandchildren, Sarah Anne Valente,
and the child in me.
F. F.

For my mother, Lillian, and my father, William.
M. M.

A comprehensive children's workbook for "A Gull's Story" and the Jersey Shore is available to download for free at www.jerseyshorevacation.com.

ISBN 0-9632906-3-0
Library of Congress Control Number: 2001097483

Printed and bound in Hong Kong
First Edition, April 2002

The typefaces used are: Americana, Avant Garde, and Stone Serif.
The paper is Shinmorrim A-2 Matt Coated, wt. 157gsm.

Jersey Shore Publications
Publishers of:
  Books:
    To The Shore Once More
    To The Shore Once More, Volume II
    Dick LaBonté, Paintings Of The Jersey Shore And More
    Spring Lake, Revisited
  Magazines and Guide Books:
    Jersey Shore Vacation Magazine
    Jersey Shore Vacation Map
    The Jersey Shore Guide Book
    Jersey Shore Home & Garden

Editor and Publisher: George C. Valente
Post Office Box 176, Bay Head, New Jersey 08742-0176
Telephone: 732-892-1276 • Fax: 732-892-3365
www.jerseyshorevacation.com

A Gull's Story

A Tale of Learning about Life, the Shore, and the ABCs

written by Frank Finale • illustrated by Margie Moore

Along the Jersey Shore, as it has been for thousands of years, lives a family of Gulls.

Mama Gull, Papa Gull, and Baby Gull rested comfortably on the moonlit sandy beach, sleeping to the sounds of gently breaking waves along the shore. *Swooooshhhhhh…Swooooshhhhhh.*

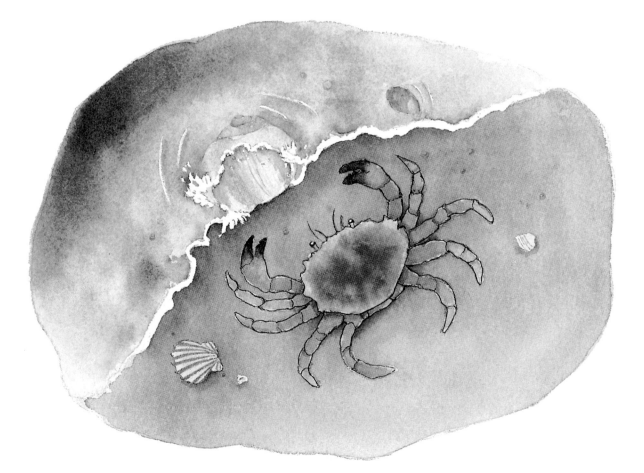

As the first rays of the morning sun beamed over the horizon, Mama Gull awoke and mewed, "Wake up, Baby Gull, wake up! Today is a special day!"

Baby Gull yawned, flitted along the sand, and cried, "What is it, what is it?"

"Today, Baby Gull, is the day you learn about where we live and your ABCs," Mama Gull said and smiled.

"And maybe a few lessons more," Papa Gull added. "Just as we have learned."

Baby Gull, happy for the adventures to come, excitedly flew up and soared over the blue-green breakers. Papa Gull and Mama Gull followed in the rainbow of colors in the sunrise sky and joined Baby Gull above the sea.

"**A** is for the **Atlantic Ocean**, where we began our lives," Mama Gull said. "The **Atlantic** is mother to us all." Papa Gull **agreed** and said, "**Appreciate** who you are."

"**B** is for **Barnegat Lighthouse**, sometimes called 'Old **Barney**.'
Your great, great grandfather flew and perched here, watching
clipper ships sail by. Remember your family history," Papa Gull said.

"**C** is for **crabs**, who **crawl** in our bays and ocean. **Crabs** are good to eat, but watch their **claws** so you don't get pinched!"

"**D** is for **dunes** and the **dune grasses** that hold them in place. Without the **dune grass**, much of our beach would be washed away," Mama Gull said, as Baby Gull perched on a piece of **driftwood** and looked at a **dragonfly**.

"**E** is for the **egret** by the **eel grass** in the **estuary** looking for something to **eat**."

"**F** is for the red **fox** searching for **fish** in the **fisherman's** pail."

"**G** is for **Gull Island**, where we visit every now and then. Sometimes at night, the **great horned owl** flies out here looking for mice."

"**H** is for **horseshoe crabs**, whose **home** is the shallow waters along the Atlantic Coast. Many times Papa and I watched **hundreds** coming ashore laying their eggs in the sand."

"**I** is for **inlet**, an opening in the land that connects the ocean and bay. It's one of our favorite places to fish and fly," said Papa Gull. "Let your wings and **imagination** soar."

"**J** is for the **Jersey Devil**, a mythical winged creature with a horse's head, a vulture's claws, and a dragon's tail that people say roams the Pine Barrens. If you ever see him, **jump**!"

"**K** is for the tiny **killifish**," said Mama Gull. Their quick schools flash in the sun. Look! The crested **kingfisher** is ready to dive!"

"**L** is for **lighthouses** that brighten the shore. From Sandy Hook to Cape May, these **landmarks** once **lit** the way home for many a sailor."

"**M** is for **monarchs** that **migrate** along the shore all the way down to **Mexico**. Always be on the lookout for life's little **miracles**," **Mama Gull** remarked.

"**N** is for **night** and the **new** light each morning brings. 'N' is also for the shell **necklaces** that the children wear as they walk the tideline."

"**O** is for two great hunters, the **osprey** and the **owl**. The **osprey** hunts the **ocean** by day. The **owl** hunts the land by night. Both are keen **observers** of what they see and hear," Papa Gull said.

"**P** is for **pitch pines** that live in the salt-wind by the shore," Papa Gull said. Mama Gull added, "See how the **passing** wind **plays** with their needled branches? Always set aside time to **play**."

"**Q** is for **quahog**. From these hard clam shells that clutter the beach, the Lenni-Lenape Indians made wampum beads."

"**R** is for the **red fox**, the **rabbit**, the **raccoon**, and the **red-winged blackbird** who use the tall **reeds** by the **river** for **rest**. **Remember**, **rest** is important," Papa Gull said.

"**S** is for the **sleek stingray** who glides along the bottom of the **sea**."

"**T** is for **tide pools** left behind when the **tide** is out. Each has its own **tiny** world of sea life. **Take** the **time** to look."

"**U** is for **underwater**. Hold your breath and look at the magical world beneath the waves, but be careful of the **undertow**."

"**V** is for **vacations** at the Jersey Shore. Families come here to swim in the ocean and stay in **Victorian** houses by the sea."

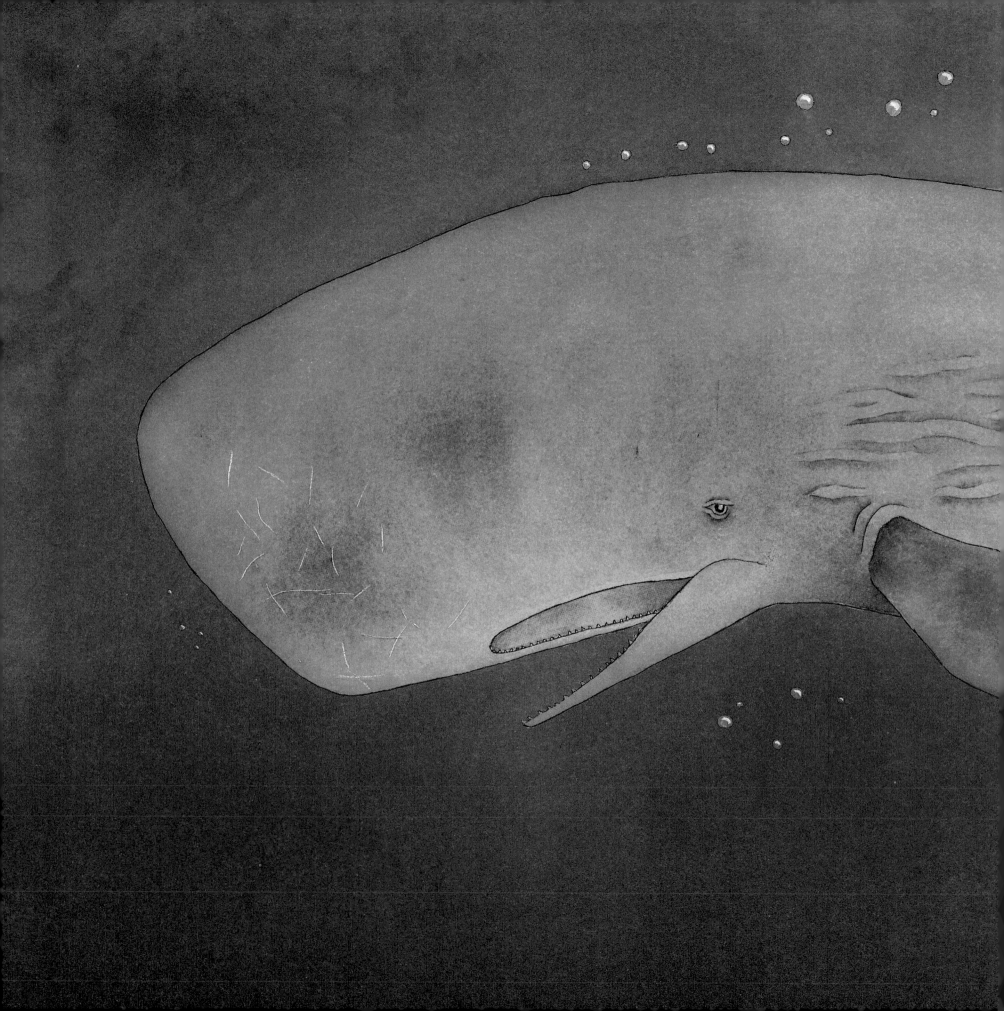

"W is for whale, the world's biggest mammal. It breathes through its blowhole and must come up for air. People of all ages enjoy whale watching."

"**X** is for 'X **marks the spot**' for buried treasure! It is said that the pirate Captain Kidd buried his treasure somewhere on the shore. People see the 'X' on a treasure map, but we can see it from the sky!" Papa Gull mewed.

"**Y** is for **yachts** that fun-loving people sail on the rivers, bays, and ocean. 'Y' is also for **yawn**, the sound we make at the end of the day when we are tired from our adventures."

"**Z** is for 'ZZZZZZZZzzzzzzzz', the sound of sleep that we make after a day of learning and fun at the shore. Sleep well, Baby Gull. Dream of the moon and stars."

The next morning, as the sun's rays flashed over the sea, the Gull family awoke.

Together, they flew in the dawn's new light, soaring in happy circles over the shore, ready once again for the day's adventures.

GLOSSARY

Atlantic Ocean – The large body of salt water that lies along the east coast of America.

eel grass – An underwater plant that has long, narrow leaves.

estuary – The place at the mouth of a river where the river's current meets the sea's tide.

horseshoe crabs – Not crabs at all! They are related to spiders and have not changed in millions of years. They are found only on the Atlantic Coast.

killifish – Small fishes sometimes used by fishermen to catch bigger fish.

landmark – A building or object on land that one can easily recognize.

Lenni-Lenape Indians – The name of the Indians who first lived in New Jersey.

migrate – To go from one country or region to another, repeatedly and in a large group, as do certain birds and butterflies.

miracle – A wonder; an extraordinary happening.

mythical – Based on a made-up story about something that can not be proven.

observe – To look at something closely.

osprey – A large, fish-eating hawk.

Pine Barrens – A forest in southern and central New Jersey with many small pine trees, sandy soils, and swampy streams.

undertow – The underwater pull that happens after waves break on the shore.

Victorian house – A type of house that was popular during the time of Queen Victoria of England, 1837-1901.

wampum – Beads made of polished shells that were used as money by the Indians.